How Strong Is an Ant?

BY KURT WALDENDORF

Published by The Child's World®
1980 Lookout Drive • Mankato, MN 56003-1705
800-599-READ • www.childsworld.com

Photographs ©: Eric Isselee/Shutterstock Images, cover, 1, 10;
Shutterstock Images, 2–3, 4–5, 6, 8–9, 9, 16–17, 12, 18, 20–21, 23;
Kirsanov Valeriy Vladimirovich/Shutterstock Images, 7; Scott
Harms/iStockphoto, 10–11; iStockphoto, 12–13; Andrey Pavolv/
Shutterstock Images, 15; Nixx Photography/Shutterstock
Images, 16; Neil Roy Johnson/Shutterstock Images, 18–19

ISBN 9781503816817
LCCN 2016945856

Printed in the United States of America
PA02325

ABOUT THE AUTHOR

Kurt Waldendorf is a writer and editor.
He lives in Vermont with his wife and their
Old English sheepdog, Charlie.

NOTE FOR PARENTS AND TEACHERS

The Child's World® helps early readers develop their informational-reading skills by providing easy-to-read books that fascinate them and hold their interest. Encourage new readers by following these simple ideas:

BEFORE READING

- Page briefly through the book. Discuss the photos. What does the reader think he or she will learn in this book? Let the child ask questions.
- Look at the glossary together. Discuss the words.

READ THE BOOK

- Now read the book together, or let the child read the book independently.

AFTER READING

- Urge the child to think more. Ask questions such as, "What things are different among the animals shown in this book?"

An ant is small but strong. How strong is an ant?

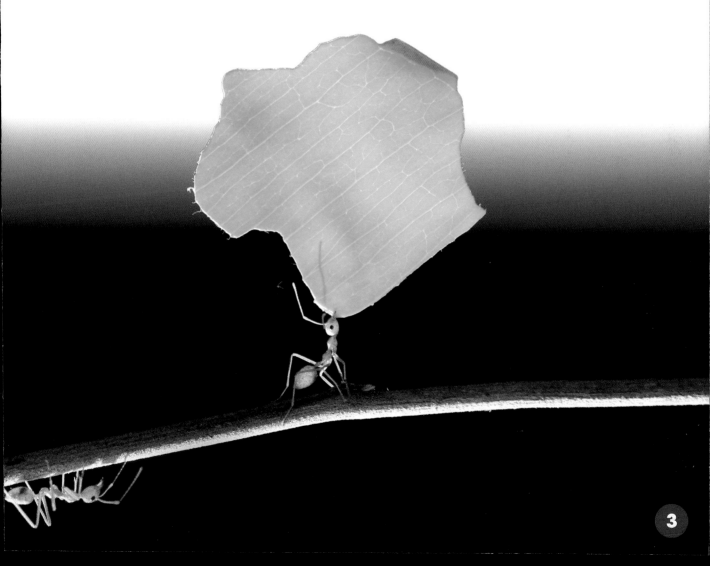

Ants collect food for their **colony**. One ant can lift the weight of 50 other ants.

Ants work together to lift bigger objects.

Eight ants could carry one grasshopper.

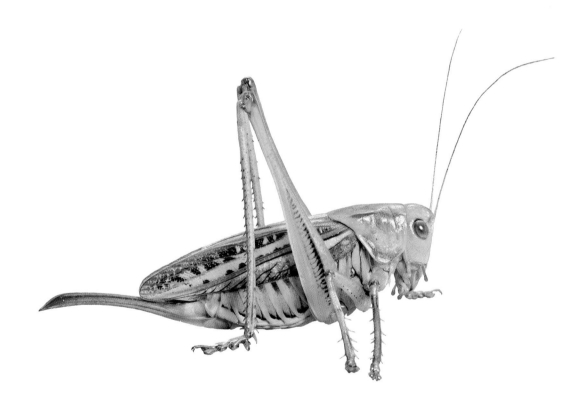

Sometimes objects get in an ant's way.

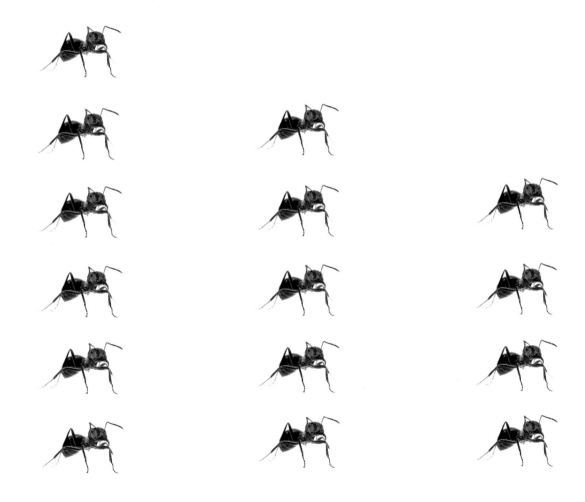

About 20 ants could lift
an acorn out of the way.

Thousands of ants live in a colony. It would take about 100 ants to carry a small bird.

Ants can use their jaws to push off the ground and jump. If a person had the same strength, he or she could jump over a four-story house.

13

If a human were as strong as an ant, he or she could lift a large van.

An ant has a strong, **sturdy** neck. It allows an ant to hold the weight of a spoon.

Strong legs help ants work quickly. If ants were the size of humans, they could run faster than a racehorse.

Sometimes ants need to cross over a gap. Ants use their bodies to make a bridge. That is strong!

CHECK IT OUT!

- An ant is one of the world's strongest animals for its size.

- Ants have different jobs within the colony.

- Ants live everywhere on Earth except Antarctica.

- In many colonies, a single queen ant lays all the eggs.

- Queen ants can live for up to 30 years.

- There are more than 12,000 ant **species**.

- Ants have been around since the time of the dinosaurs.

colony (KAH-luh-nee) A colony is a large group of animals that live together. Many ants form a single colony.

species (SPEE-sheez) A species is one group that the same animals and plants are divided into. There are many different species, or kinds, of ants.

sturdy (STUR-dee) Something is sturdy if it is strong or solidly built. An ant has a sturdy neck that helps it lift things.

TO LEARN MORE

BOOKS

Abbott, Henry. *Inside Anthills*.
New York, NY: PowerKids Press, 2015.

Aronin, Miriam. *The Ant's Nest*.
New York, NY: Bearport, 2017.

Spilsbury, Louise. *Survival of the Fittest*.
New York, NY: Gareth Stevens, 2015.

WEB SITES

Visit our Web site for links about ants: **childsworld.com/links**

Note to Parents, Teachers, and Librarians: We routinely verify our Web links to make sure they are safe and active sites. So encourage your readers to check them out!

INDEX